Please note:

The UK and USA share the English lang[...] [...]
words that are spelled differently. Some words have extra letters in the British spelling, such as the word cancelled. In American English, it is spelled canceled. There are also words that interchange the letters c or s and sometimes z. For example, in America, you spell offense and in Britain, it is written as offence.

Examples of words you'll see in the book include: kerb, litre, centre, manoeuver, travelling and colour.

These spellings are **not** incorrect.

This book is written in UK English to reflect my Australian/English background.

Sexy Sassy Romance is only a click away!

Newsletter Sign Up

https://imogenenix.net/newsletter-2/

CHAPTER 1

I'd love to say this entire disaster was caused by my father, but sadly enough, I can't. I'm sitting on the floor, in a wedding gown, looking at a smashed cake and wondering how it all went so wrong. "Come on Amanda," I tell myself, but it doesn't really make me feel any better about the mess that meets my gaze.

There's no tears and certainly no regrets. After all, when Charlie walked out on me an hour or so ago, he made the whole situation pretty damned clear.

"You were told this had to work, Amanda. I warned you I wouldn't stay if you couldn't commit to keeping that dog out of this today. So, what did you do? Ignored me!"

Charlie, my best friend, neighbour and a whole heap more had slammed his way from the building. Those watching had hemmed and hawed before leaving too. Meanwhile, Brutus, my pup now snuffled at the cake which lay shattered and scattered on the floor.

"Not my finest hour, Brutus."

Hell, he was a Cavalier King Charles Spaniel and my best bud and the last present from my father. He'd hung in there when Dad had finally passed away three months ago, from cancer. He'd stayed with me on the nights when I couldn't come to terms with the truth that I was alone.

I pushed up off the floor, calling Brutus to me. He rose and whined, no doubt read the distress that rolled off me in waves.

"Come on boy, let's go home." I'd need to change back into my daggy jeans and button up shirt. Leaving the gown behind, itchy tag and all, would be a pleasure.

Retreating to the dressing room I reached for the millions of tiny buttons. It was only then I realised, I couldn't reach them. I sighed and recognised, being alone really sucked.

I mean, great big hairy balls, kind of sucked.

"Hey, anyone out there?" I couldn't help but hope someone had stayed behind during the disaster of the photo shoot, but after a couple of minutes, my repeat of calling for assistance, there was nothing. Nada. Not a sound.

My clothes still hung on the hooks where I'd hung them and looking around, I knew, Brutus and I were all alone and I was still dressed in the gown I was supposed to be modelling.

My phone beeped. I scooped it up, hoping to ring Charlie and make my apologies but it blinked the 'battery empty' icon then died.

"Noooo!"

Brutus cried and scurried to the end of the change room and I inhaled. Nice and deep, letting that oxygen fill my lungs and hopefully bring with it some kind of emotional cleansing. "Nope," I muttered and leaned down. Clearly, Brutus and I would have to drive home in this poufy confection.

"Won't that look fine?" I clipped Brutus' lead on and on a sigh, gathered up my clothes, bag and now flat phone. The keys, thankfully on one of those lanyard things were easy to find. I shuffled stuff around to fit as much as I could into my bag and shoved my way out of the building.

Tromping down the street, in a wedding gown, my hair still adorned with speckles of cake icing, duffle over my shoulder and leading Brutus wasn't how I'd planned for the day to go. *Hell, did any bride?* People looked at me, giving me the 'what the fuck is going on,' look. I felt more than bloody self-conscious right now. At least my model training came into its own. I marched down that street like I owned it, except the whole time I felt I should be squirming with embarrassment.

I should be good at this stuff. Given my lack of husband right now... Much as I wanted to shy from the truth, I really was a stuff up in the love and romance department. Kind of like my latest photo shoot.

Squaring my shoulders, I kept going as memories of all my stuff ups before rotated through my mind.

My last boyfriend, Tex—and yeah, that was his name—told me I had commitment issues. He could be right, but then again, maybe he wasn't. After all, we'd been a 'thing' for nearly six months, and it had come to a head after he'd gone back to the US to sort out his best friend's ranch. In hindsight, maybe I had used it as an excuse to end it all but something about the relationship felt forced.

The guy before him, Marty, had actually proposed. The engagement lasting three weeks before I'd run away. Sure, I'd told him my trip to Majorca was for a calendar shoot—which it had—the only thing is he'd seen my social media posts and those of the other models. Me getting cosy with the Latin guy they'd hired to make us look good hadn't gone over so well.

At my car, I stopped, inserted the key and ushered Brutus in.

He settled in the back seat and I fastened his seat belt. "Gotta keep you safe," I whispered.

I tossed my bag on the passenger seat and slid in behind the wheel. The gown slid up, nearly choking me with layers of ruffles, petticoats and lace and I had to push it down and hope it wouldn't get in the way of driving.

My car started, sounding like a wheezing cougar. "I really need to get it serviced," I muttered and checked my rear-view mirror.

A tiny car, one of those hybrid deals appeared and I closed my eyes. Not what I needed right now.

Charlie parked and climbed out. I watched him in the mirror, the long stalk as he prowled toward me.

As always, just seeing him made my stomach jumble and skip.

If only...

Frustration as always scoured me when dealing with Amanda. It wasn't that we'd argued. I couldn't. She was... I shied away from that thought, because right now, bright red traffic lights flashed in my mind warning me that thinking those things only led to a lot more disappointment.

Amanda's car wheezed. She hadn't yet got it serviced, even after I'd reminded her and when I finally reached the car door and stared down at her, I noted the mascara dribbles and the fact she was still wearing that damned gown. As always, the urge to fix her problems rose. Unhealthy, I reminded myself and strengthened my emotional barriers, but as always they wobbled around her.

She wound down the window, her lip quivering.

"Going somewhere?"

She sighed, closed her eyes and for a moment I was thankful. Those soft gray eyes got to me every time. "Home. I was going home."

"Hmm, in the gown?" I kept my voice light, not wanting to scare her. She'd fly if I didn't step carefully.

"Well, everyone else had gone. I tried but..."

"I'll follow you. We need to talk, anyway." I backed away before she could say anything else. I didn't want to hear how she was sorry. It really wasn't her fault and I knew that. She'd tried to find a sitter for Brutus but at such short notice I'd agreed to let her bring him. He'd created havoc at her place. Eaten pillows and chewed on shoes. Had a predilection to her lipstick and would snuffle through her discarded handbags then crunch on the cases until he reached the pink and red gooey sticks.

I also needed to apologise for my ill thought out words. I'd seen the way she flinched. Brutus was the last present given to her by her father. He'd been there during the worst of her grief and I'd been too short. Too curt. Too angry to consider my words.

Climbing into my car I reversed, giving her the space she needed to manoeuvre, then followed her home, wincing everytime the car let out a puff of black smoke.

I remembered, vividly the day she'd bought it.

"Why did you buy that piece of junk?" I stalked into the garage and she turned to face me. Her face wreathed in smiles as she bounced her way over to me.

"Dad said he drove one in high school. I like it anyway. It looks like a guy magnet." The bright white of her teeth flashed, and her eyes sparkled.

"It's not sensible," I started to yell, then kept the rest of my thoughts to myself. 'She doesn't need a guy magnet. She's already one!'

Amanda frowned, "But Charlie, I'm a model. I need something flashy and I could afford it."

Sighing my frustration, I peered inside. "How much did you pay?"

With a broad smile she told me, and my stomach sank to my ankles. She'd been ripped off once more.

"It's going to need work," I offered, and she nodded.

"I know. But Dad says he knows someone." The words just tripped from her lips and much as I couldn't stand it when she got that hopeful look in her eyes, I could only shrug. After all, her Dad was her biggest supporter.

Even now, I looked back on that day, and wondered why I hadn't said something to her. "Because you know she's soft and you didn't want to hurt her, asshole."

We turned into her street. At the end sat the tiny bungalow where she'd been raised by her father after her mother left.

She hadn't changed anything about the house since her father died and not for the first time, I wondered how she was getting on, emotionally. Oh, don't get me wrong, she's got money enough to afford to do what she wants. Amanda's a successful model, but the day to day stuff isn't her forte and clearing out her father's things would be tough.

She met me at the door, and not for the first time today, the shock of her in a wedding gown almost blew my mind.

If I'd been dressing her, it would be a mermaid shape, with wisps fluttering at her feet and the rest of it moulding itself to her delicious curves. The fluffy cake topper they'd dressed her in was all wrong for her shape.

"Come on in," she invited, and I followed Amanda through the tiny alcove and into the lounge.

The room was untidy, with cups and magazines lying on surfaces that should have them. "I'm not..." she fluttered her hands and turned. "Can you undo me please?"

My fingers found the millions of tiny seed pearl-like buttons. I'd dreamed of this on more than one occasion, my unbuttoning her out of a wedding gown. My body reacted the way it always does. Turning painfully hard immediately.

Shifting on my feet, I hoped she wouldn't notice and as usual she didn't. *Thankfully.*

The gown slid to the floor and she stepped out of it.

It took every ounce of willpower to ignore the almost naked woman, standing there in tiny panties, strapless bra and six-inch heels.

"What's wrong with me?" During my introspection, Amanda had turned back to face me, and I let my gaze settle on her face. If I looked anywhere else...

On a sigh, I refocussed my thoughts. "What do you mean?"

She tottered to the armchair and slumped down. I tried really hard to ignore the bobble of her breasts as she moved. Not that I did too well because that pain in my groin? It was like a shooting stick of hunger pain.

"Well, I'm good looking, right? A model, for fricks sake. I'm single and live with a dog who I can't even find a sitter for. I'm doing a favour for my best friend, by showcasing his designs and I mess it up. Why? Why do I always do these things?"

My gut lurched. You know, the way your belly feels like it's wobbling from side to side in emotionally charged situations? Yes, it did just that! I found the other armchair and slid down.

"You're just..." I hunted for the right words. "You're accident prone. Life isn't cut and dried for everyone, Amanda. Sometimes our abilities are more on the—"

"Aesthetic side. Look I've heard that before," she growled and I gaped at her.

"I've never said that about you!" The words shot from my mouth and she frowned.

"No. You've always made excuses for me, covered up or helped me sift and sort through the issues." She swiped an unsteady hand over her eyes. "Why?" Her voice assumed the fragile shaky variety and my gut clenched.

I locked the answer down quick and hard. If I told her, she'd run a million miles away, just like she did with every other poor sap who showed some kind of true romantic interest in her.

"That's what friends do." It was the best I could offer.

"Friends. Yep. Okay, so you said you needed to talk."

I jerked at the way Amanda changed the subject. "Oh, uh… Yeah. Look I've been offered the chance of a lifetime. A six-page spread in 'Brides of the Northern Hemisphere'. I need a model. Not in a gown that looks like some kind of cake topper, but wearing the rings I design, for their Summer Showpiece. I want you to model them for me."

She gaped. "I'm… I mean, this was a favour and I've messed it up. Why?"

"Because you're perfect." I couldn't call the words back fast enough to undo what I'd just said. I closed my eyes and counted. *Nuh unh.* I'd still said them.

Charlie *called me perfect.* God knew, I needed those words today. I needed them from *him.* Just not quite like this.

I'd been crushing on him since I was like eleven and he'd been fourteen and the cute boy next door.

"So, you want me to model your rings?" I said, feeling downright stupid in bra, panties and heels. He'd barely looked at me and I wondered if he ever would.

Over the last three years, I'd jumped into relationships at will, more than a little aware that he'd been dating Sabrina, followed by Kiersten then Layla. All of them beautiful, accomplished and 'together'. He liked women who had their lives under control and wasn't that just the polar opposite from me? I couldn't even find Brutus a dog sitter, keep the house clean or balance my accounts.

I pushed up from my seat, suddenly furious. Why? Well, I don't actually know. I reached for the clasp of my bra as he watched. Some seed of devilry urging me on as I unclipped it.

It fell to the ground and my breasts sprang free. I sighed and stretched, more than a little aware that he was staring. If this had been a cartoon his eyeballs would be popping out on stalks.

God knew, this was the last throw of the dice. If he didn't show some kind of interest in me being damned forward, well, I'd give up modelling and… and… open a bookstore. Dad always said I was made for books. I had more than enough in my room and the storage shed downtown was bulging at the sides from the many titles Dad and I had read.

"Uh Amanda?"

"Yes?" Waiting was clawing at my senses. I wanted him. I always had. Surely this time…?

"You took off your bra." He sounded strangled.

I hooked my hands in my panties and started to slip them down as he lurched from the seat. "Wait."

I kept my thumb and fingers still as he reached out.

"So?" My voice wobbled.

"Will you help me?" The words sounded like a moan.

It was almost as if he couldn't control himself and the look on his face when those words slid out surprised me.

"What?" His voice slid out coating my nerves with delicious hunger.

I groaned. "Charlie…" God, I was making all kinds of fool of myself. Either he'd take the bait or not.

"Mandy," he whispered, and tears pricked my eyes. *Mandy*. That's what he'd called me that summer I'd realised he was a boy and I was a girl and the emotion fairy had made her delivery of hormones. It was like a shock of frigid water. He still thought of me as that little girl. It froze my ardour like an ice cube in the freezer

I slid my hands free. "I'll just go grab my wrap." I tottered away. Too little. Too late.

Sliding my fingers through my hair, I tug. "I've fucked up."

I'd seen that look in her eyes. God knew my body was freaking aching to hold her. Touch her and dammit yes, fuck her. But she meant too much more for me to do it when she was at rock bottom.

I stalked from one end of the room to the other. "Fucking fool!"

"Who?" Her voice echoed through me and I turned. She'd cinched the belt of the short robe tight.

"Me." The word slipped out.

Her eyes widened. "You've never been a fool. You drive a sensible car. The women you date are at the top of their fields and fabulous. You've got a successful jewellery business."

A harsh laugh ripped from my throat. She didn't even scratch the surface and maybe that was the problem. I locked her away from the realities of my life.

The one I'd rather share with her. On a leap of faith, I advanced. "I drive a hybrid because it's environmentally friendly and cheap to run. I have a business I love but it's successful because I hired well, and my staff keep me in line. I date women who don't remind me of you, because it's easier than asking and being told no."

Her face paled and I knew it. Just fucking knew I'd destroyed any chances I had with her. Instead of waiting to be told to leave, I turned and stalked to the door. "Ring me and let me know if you'll do the job for me."

I needed out of there. Quickly.

CHAPTER 2

*A*fter Charlie left, I stood there. Reeling from what he'd just told me. He didn't want to be told no. By me?

The gown sat abandoned on the floor, still covered in cake and frosting. Brutus had curled up in the middle of it, making it into a dog bed. Brutus wasn't picky, so long as it was soft and comfy. I bent down and picked up the caramel and white dog off the dress. "I have to return this," I murmured, but the world had tilted on its axis.

All because of Charlie.

He'd left and that felt like it was crushing me. I hurried for the door, Brutus under my arms in time to see him zooming off up street. The heavy sigh didn't make me feel any better. Nor did Charlie's mum, scurrying out the front door and waving to me. "Was that Charlie? I need to give him the recipe he asked for. Layla wants to make my soda bread for her grandmother."

When Mrs Campbell stopped and looked at me, there was pity on her face. "Oh dear, what happened Mandy?" She stepped forward and I stood aside, letting her inside the house.

She was the first, apart from Charlie since Dad died and I knew the minute the mess I'd left met her gaze.

"Mandy?" She bent and picked up the discarded wedding gown.

"I… It was a modelling shoot. The one Charlie was helping me with. Brutus knocked the cake over, thankfully after we'd finished the photos."

Mrs Campbell cocked her head to one side. "And?"

"Charlie got angry and drove off."

The woman wound her arms about me, and I let the warmth and affection flood me. "Then I did something really stupid."

"What, dear?"

My head spun because, dammit, the warmth of her hug, the almost motherly way she'd read that I needed someone to talk to, reminded me that my own mother hadn't wanted this responsibility. The understanding pounded into me. If I pushed away, she'd be hurt, though understanding, but I couldn't do that. Not this time. We'd been through this routine before, so I merely shook my head. "I tried to seduce him."

She held still; Charlie's mum, then started to laugh. "And?"

I blushed. *Did I really tell her that?*

"He didn't… We didn't…" Oh. My. God. I need to learn to control my mouth.

"I've known you since you were born, Mandy dear. I know my son too and what he wants. If he didn't take you up, there's a reason. One I don't know, but I do know he's wanted you for a long time. You're going to have to chase him if you want him, though."

I blinked and pulled away. "Chase him?"

Mrs Campbell nodded. "Yes, dear. He's shy and unsure. Besides, his father and I have been waiting for years. So did your dad."

The words were like a peal of bells. Too loud. Too much. "Waiting?" I sounded like a twit, repeating her words, but I needed to make sure I really understood clearly. "Chase him?"

"Of course. Now, you're not a silly girl and not normally so clueless, but I'll cut you a break and tell you more later. Right now though, it appears you need a cleaner. As for where Charlie is concerned, he's only been seeing these women because they're safe. They aren't looking for a husband, not really. They're your complete opposite so he's emotionally protected."

If I'd suddenly turned cross-eyed and toothless, you couldn't have surprised me more.

Mrs Campbell headed for the front door. "I'll be back in a minute with the number for Julia Henscliffe. She's a great cleaner, and Selina uses her too. Then you and I need to have a chat. Oh and getting dressed might help too."

She was gone and once more, there I stood alone. Confused, while my hands clutched the edges of my wrap. "How the hell did I get in this mess?" There just wasn't an answer.

At my sister Selina's house, I stopped the car and sat in it on the driveway. She'd be home, looking after her month-old twins, Netta and Riley. When I saw the curtains twitch, I also knew she'd caught on that I was parked there. With a groan I climbed from the car and tottered to the door. Tottered because my head was still swirling at the fact that I'd walked away from the most beautiful girl in the world and that she'd told me she wanted me. Propositioned me even!

Hot fucking damn.

I'm such a moron.

Selina opened the door, and peered toward me. "Come on in," she whispered, and I followed her in. I'd been warned after the babies were born, that if I turned up and they were asleep any conversation would be super quiet.

"Asleep?"

She nodded and ushered me to the dining room, picking up a tiny device I knew to be the baby monitor in her hand.

We sat at the table and she placed the tiny unit on the table between us. "Mum rang. Said you'd run off after some kind of head on clash with Mandy."

I shook my head, because really, there was still the vestiges of fog invading my mind. "I nearly jumped her, Sel."

My sister leaned forward, her face lighting up. "And?"

I shrugged. "I stuffed up. Walked out."

Her mouth grew into a large 'o' before she blinked. "You're a fool. You've only been wanting her for like half your life. I remember the summer you were fourteen and trying to make out she wasn't the girl you planned to marry, until you said she was."

I remember that conversation like it only just took place. And yes, I did actually say that, in the end. Instead of letting the memory take me though, I rubbed my eyes. "I also asked her to model the rings for the bridal magazine special."

Now her gaze turned to full of pity and she reached out, taking my hand. "You're going to let her wear it?"

The ring. The one I'd fashioned for her. The one that had sealed my life change from Journeyman jeweller to Master Craftsman.

Set in platinum, it featured a single asscher diamond, the band studded with ruby chips. I'd made it for her to wear. Not that I guessed she ever would.

"Yeah, probably." I shrugged, trying to make out that it didn't bother me, but deep down the desire for her to wear my ring for the rest of her life grew daily.

"You know, you could just do the deed with her. Then see where that takes you." Selina grinned and I stared at her. My baby sister, five years younger than me, though married and mother of two, was suggesting I should involve myself in mindless sex with the woman I loved?"

"Uh, no thanks." I'd already made enough of a mistake in handling the situation with her. I really didn't need to make things worse and implode any chance we had left of making it work.

"You've got nothing to lose, Charlie. Mum says she's upset and ripe for the picking."

I blinked. "Mum said that?"

"Well, not in those words, but it's what she meant."

I squeezed my eyes shut. "Mad house," I muttered, and she tittered until the sounds of a baby's cry filled the air.

She shot up out of the chair. "Gotta go feed the babies. Let yourself out and make sure you lock the door as you go."

Then she was gone, and I was looking at the tablecloth and wondering how the hell my life got this complicated.

I guess it all started when Mandy's parents bought the house next door. I don't remember that, because according to mum I was only two or three months old. Mandy was a 'born early' baby and the strain of mothering a preemie was too much for her mother. She'd cut and run when Mandy was a toddler. Mandy's paternal grandmother had moved in with them until Mandy went to school.

It was just them after that, but they'd been close and full of life and fun. When Mandy was fifteen, she'd been spotted shopping by a talent scout in the shopping centre. Since then, her life had become a whirl. She'd been on covers of magazines, in the odd commercial and most recently the face of a major cosmetic deal.

"But she still lived at home," I said to the empty room then stood and headed for the door.

Why? She could be living the high life on the continent, have a house in New York and an apartment in LA yet she stayed here, in the pokey little village where we'd grown up.

Sure, she'd been engaged and dated. A lot. I'd remembered meeting Tex and Phil and even her ex-fiancé Marty. They'd been nice. Larger than life but she'd run every time commitment raised its head. Never staying long enough to let them capture her with a gold wedding band.

Tex had even questioned me as to why she'd stayed here, when she could be living the high life and to be honest, I hadn't been able to answer because it confused me too.

I guess if Amanda didn't want that, it confused me further why she chose them and not me? I could offer her stability, love. A home.

Why?

By the time I made it home to my flat, my head ached, but at least the fire in my groin had settled.

Mrs Campbell returned, phone number of a sheet of paper and a bowl filled with a hearty chicken noodle soup.

"Oh, thanks," I whispered, my hair wet from a super quick shower and my face smelling like some high-priced makeup remover I'd found in my bathroom cupboard. Normally, I attended to that before leaving a shoot or event, but this time. Well, the truth was, I wasn't really thinking straight at that point. Right now, though, I'd had time to consider Mrs Campbell's words.

"Your idea that I chase Charlie. Tell me more," I said after I'd found a somewhat clean spoon from the kitchen draw.

Mrs Campbell smiled but I saw the wariness in her eyes as she looked around the kitchen. "Could I maybe wash up while we talk?"

I winced as she reached for the dishwash liquid. "I was going to put it all into the dishwasher."

"I thought it was broken?"

I bit my lip and shook my head. "I got it fixed. I just haven't filled it yet."

On a sigh, Mrs Campbell set to work, loading it up and in next to no time she sat down beside me. "I've already rung Julia and she's free tomorrow. Ring her when I leave and organise a time. Now, about Charlie... Like I said, he's shy. But I have an idea. Now listen closely...."

CHAPTER 3

*T*hree Weeks Later

I double checked the jewellery trunk one last time. The magazine had made arrangements for us to fly out with the gown designers and their precious cargo on this plane. We'd meet the cake designers on the island and even the florists who'd ordered their blooms ahead of time wandered onto the tiny jet. We had two rows of models, older, younger male and female. The only one who hadn't yet arrived was Amanda.

When she stepped aboard, ten minutes late, there were grumbles until she took the seat beside me. "I brought you some nuts," she said and passed the tiny pack to me.

I glanced at her, because she'd bought chocolate coated cashews. My favourite kind. "Uh thanks," I muttered and stashed them in my pocket, remembering the airlines warning about nuts on board. So long as they stayed in their packet, I'd be good.

"Sorry I'm late. I was picking up some essentials for the party tonight. I got all kinds of goodies," Mandy enthused, and I have to admit I was mesmerised by her infectious laugh.

It only took a few minutes and the frustrations that had filled the plane during the waiting on the tarmac melted away beneath the onslaught of Amanda at her best.

By the time we landed, we were singing all kinds of silly ditties, hands waving in the air and the models were cooing her praises.

Watching her in action never got old.

Three minibuses met us as we alighted from the plane, and they filled quickly until only one remained mostly empty. I helped her in and waited as they loaded the last of the cargo into the enclosed trailer before heading off for the hotel.

The surrounds were picturesque, and I couldn't contain myself. "That would be an awesome location for a beachside shoot," I said and pointed to the beach.

"Yes, I think it would." She nodded and smiled and the concern about out last meeting at her house weeks ago, melted away.

We stopped at a tiny glade and the driver winked. "Thought this might be a nice little side trip. Take a moment. Stretch your legs." He spoke with a lilt and I watched Mandy glory in the sound of his voice, the way her eyes sparkled, and her lips curved upwards.

The others stayed on the bus, so just Mandy and I entered the tiny green gated entry to the woods. The sound of birds chirruping, the cool greenery after the heat of the summer out there fed the well in my belly so I turned to her. "Mandy I—"

I hadn't noticed how close she crowded in until she stopped, cocked her head and smiled. "Alone. Isn't this beautiful? The perfect place…"

I opened my mouth but only a squeak emerged when she placed a single finger against my lips. "Shhhh…"

Then she kissed me.

Explosions. Fireworks. The singing of Hallelujah by choruses of angels. None of them described the feeling of his lips against mine and his tongue delving into my mouth.

Holy crap. I'd just kissed Charlie Campbell. The sexiest man alive and an artist with jewels. They weren't, however, the kind of jewels I wanted right now, though.

Heat and desire pooled low and deep in my belly.

I'd listened to Selina and Mrs Campbell's advice. Turned up late for the plane, kept everyone amused and entertained though to be honest my senses had been consumed by the man beside me. The money I'd fed the driver, so he'd stop somewhere romantic, in a quick and furtive exchange by the cargo hold paying off.

Because right here and now his arms were around me and my body was doing a little more than simply tiptoeing through the tulips. I reckon it was dancing a highland fling and hoping for the finale of the sound of music!

When he pulled away, I was panting. Hard and heavy and it gratified to see him more than a little flustered too.

"Well," I said, and he stared at me.

"Well, what?"

"That was fun," I added, and the grin filled my face.

"Yes. But Mandy…"

I reflexively winced and his shoulders dropped. "Sorry. I know you hate that name."

Shaking my head, I reached out. "It's not that I hate it. It's just… you started calling me that when I was eleven. I'm kind of over it these days."

He jolted back. "Did I?"

"Yeah." I waited a beat. "I'm not eleven anymore Charlie and I'm tired of waiting. So, here's your chance. Brutus is at home with your parents. There's nothing and no one that either of us is seeing, because I know you and Layla are over. There are no real impediments. If you want me, now is your chance."

I held my breath and waited. Was I going blue? It sure felt like the oxygen in my lungs was nearly expended before he reached out and framed my face.

"I do. But we've so much history between us."

Dammit he was going to *walk away*? That's it. Time for me to put plan b into action.

"Okay," I said and walked quickly back to the bus. Time for the game to ramp up.

Seriously, I'm not normally slow or even a dimwit. This situation though, is out of the ordinary. I mean one of the most gorgeous women in the world (or at least according to the women's magazines and their headlines) just offered herself to me and I'm standing here like a dummy. I'd just said no, basically and she'd walked away from me.

I trudged back to the bus and climbed on board. One of the other girls has nabbed my place beside Amanda, so I move into an empty seat for the rest of the ride to the hotel.

It's moody and sits on a bluff overlooking the sea. The sky, gray and wild, the sea foamy and dark and the granite of the old castle reinforces what I'm thinking. I've stuffed it and I'll die a lonely sad old man.

I climb off the bus, watching as she gathers up her carry-on bag. The trunk is offloaded, and I watch as it's carefully wheeled across the gravel drive. The value of it is immense and even in my fugue state I'm hyper aware that I have to know where it is. They're going to take it straight to the vaults, I've been told. My suitcase is shoved into my hand and I make my way inside.

There's Amanda, talking to the clerk who nods rapidly. The key changes hands and Amanda's off, up the stairs as I step up to the desk. "Charlie Campbell."

The woman smiled. "Of course, sir." I fill out her form and hand it back. She gives me a key and directions and I'm moving up the stairs in the direction Amanda took.

The building is cavernous, large and cool and I wonder what it would be like in winter, with snow settling on the ground. Probably bitter, I decide as I find my room, but also picturesque.

Thank heavens there's a fire already dancing in the hearth, given the chill of the room. There are only a few rooms in this section I'd been told, and I wonder where Amanda is. I'm not sure if I hope it's nearby, especially if she's going to participate in the sexual olympics which sometimes occur on these shoots.

I lift my suitcase onto the bed and stare at my choices. I was told to pack at least one formal outfit as the magazine traditionally holds a formal dinner during the shoot. Then I'd needed some extra shirts for contingencies, comfortable clothes and the usual toiletries and so on. I'd packed swimmers but really didn't expect the time to play. In the smaller case I'd stashed some other extra wire, a soldering iron, tools, the odd diamond and so on. If the mood took me and I had time, well, who knew?

I patted my pocket seeking the case I kept on me at all times and slid it out. Cracked the lid open and looked on the ring then on sigh closed it up. "Wishes, horses. Rich men." It doesn't do much good reminding myself, so I stash it in the bedside table.

The sound of someone knocking on the door grabs my attention and I swing it open. Amanda walks inside and closes the door.

"Okay then, I guess I have to be firm about this," she says and before I can say anything, she's opening the robe I remember so well from a couple of weeks ago.

Sliding the silky material down her arms, I'm gob-smacked because there she is wearing a pair of skimpy panties and a tiny strapless bra. Each in ruby satin as the wrap pools on the floor.

My heartbeat falters. "Oh... Mandy..."

"Really?" She mutters. "Mandy? What about Amy or Amanda? I'm standing here almost naked after I've told you why Mandy makes me feel like a randy thirteen-year-old and you can't move on?"

The snark in her voice turns my brain on. "Oh shit."

She rolls her eyes.

"Amanda, I'm..." lost of words is probably the only thing I'm capable of thinking because I want those curves so bad, my dick is almost ready to explode.

My fingers curl, without any conscious decision I reach for her, tug her close so I can feel the heat of her body through my shirt and pants.

"Let's see if we can light a fire," she whispers against my lips.

"I've got one already," then groan at the stupidity of my comment when she throws her head back and laughs.

"I can tell."

I blush and duck my head. "Amanda, I'm not sure this is such a great idea." Capturing her hands, I try to stop her before they reach the waistband and belt. "Wait. Stop."

She does, her face pale and moisture gathering in her gaze. "You don't want me."

Now it's my turn to laugh, a little mirthlessly if I'm honest. "No. That's certainly not true if you looked."

She peeked then tugged away. "What then? I'm too young, too pretty, too much an airhead?"

Before Amanda can stalk from the room, I'm spread eagled in front of the door, barring her exit. "No. Because I don't see how I can be your one. You need a man who's exciting. One who'll fit in your world."

That stopped Amanda in her tracks. Her mouth wide open and eyes staring at me.

"What does that mean?"

I rubbed my aching chest, where my shrivelled heart lay, beating only for her. "I'm boring. A jeweller. I don't have a yacht on the Caribbean or take off at a moment's notice for Nice."

"But…"

I shook my head, realising now that years of wanting have tugged me to this place where only honesty can clear the air and maybe release us from the prison we've made for ourselves. The one where she's the perfect princess and I'm the prince held in stasis by the dragon of my own making.

"You're beautiful and amazing. Men worship you from afar. You've been courted by a prince and wined by a billionaire. You've danced with a sheik and—"

"Stop. It." Her voice echoed in the room. "I didn't want them. None of them. I went out with Mikhail while you were dating Sabrina. Leora Phillips told me Sabrina was expecting you to propose. Marty during your thing with Kiersten, and it was suggested in the Times that a merger of the personal variety was pending. By the time Tex came along you'd all but shacked up with Layla and I was there when your mother was about to hand over the recipe for her soda bread." Her voice rose with each woman's name, so it chimed loudly enough to break through the pain that radiated inside my chest.

"What?"

Anguish filled her face. "I didn't want them. Every man was to fill the void that was empty because I couldn't have you." Tears dribbled down her face. My gut ached as did my heart.

"Shit!"

I suck at telling people things they're not ready to hear, just like I suck at listening to hard truths. When Dad got sick and the doctors told me it was terminal, I kept up the pretence until there could be no denying it.

When I broke up with Marty, I made sure he saw pics of me on Social Media because I was too much of a coward to tell him to his face that I'd made another dreadful mistake by saying yes.

I'm not really the airhead most people think, but I know in my heart, I've filled my life with vacuous pursuits because I'm afraid.

Terrified of the truth: of being alone and even worse, that one day I'll come home and find Charlie married to some deserving little woman who makes him happy with three tiny perfect children. But I needed to stay in the vicinity too, like a magnet drawn to shards of metal.

It was why we've remained friends, I guess. I couldn't let him go no matter that is was probably really unfair to him. I'd needed to be part of his life, because I'm like a bloody limpet.

We'd continued to circle in the same people and business. Him a jeweller of renown. He'd even made the ring for a certain princess on her engagement. Me? I'd only pretended to be a princess in a circular or weekly gossip rag.

I might be on the cover of magazines, but he made the stuff that women salivate over. He's gorgeous at six foot two, with dark brown hair, green eyes and the face of an angel. I know people think I'm perfect because of my blonde hair, grey eyes and curvy figure and at six one, I'm tall enough to be a model because it come naturally, but without him? It's pretty hollow.

He's an artist with metal and jewels. Me? I'm merely the statue they show it on. A blank canvas.

"Damn it, Amanda. I have always wanted you. That summer I turned fourteen? I told Selina I'd marry you, someday. You'd already started to grow and fill, but even more than that, you had a sweet heart and a loving nature and I wanted that. For the rest of my life."

Those words stopped me. I felt oxygen starved and stared at him. "No, you felt sorry for me. The other girls were being mean, teasing and—"

"Trust me," I added drily, "no boy ever had as many wet dreams as I did that summer."

The words speared me. Then a spear of humour took root. "Really?" I lifted my eyes to his.

"Yeah. Dad had to give me the talk, cause mum was beside herself. She had to wash my pyjamas pretty much every day that summer." A tinge of pink coloured his cheeks.

"I'm… uh…." *What does a girl say to that?* Thanks, didn't really seem to fit the bill, so I stayed quiet but smiled.

He came closer, crowding me. "I have always wanted you. I still want you. I will probably always want you."

Oh. My. God. Those last words he whispered against my mouth and the sudden sweet breath fanned against sensitized skin.

If I moved, not even an inch, we'd kiss.

I wanted it. Badly.

Closing the distance, I rested my hands on the heat and strength of his shoulders. Curled them around so the feel of his sinews and bones which anchored me. If they didn't, I'm sure I'd float right up to the ceiling.

His lips closed on mine, full and plump, firm and warm. Fires licked inside my belly and I wanted to dance in them. To give in to the hunger that roared inside my veins.

His tongue found its way into my mouth and the emptiness in my abdomen spread, like licking tongues of hunger.

The groan that tore from him filled the need in me and the kiss deepened, while his hands slid over my shoulders, bare and quivering beneath his careful touch.

"Touch me," I demanded, and his hand skated down my arm and the when it settled on my back, the feeling was electric. My body quivered like never before, and that throbbing between my legs? I wanted only him to fill it with an urgency I'd never before known.

I reached back and unfastened my bra. Tugging the ruby satin off my body and this time, he cupped one aching full breast and I couldn't stop the sound of sheer delight that echoed in the room.

"So beautiful," he crooned and dipped his head. The touch of his breath upon my nipple sent a shot of lightning down to my most secret areas and my legs shook.

"Please," I implored, and he slid his mouth over the nub.

At this rate, I was going to come before he even got into my panties, I thought, frantic and hungry.

"Slow down," Charlie whispered but it took every ounce of will power not to push him to the floor, strip him naked and ride him like a bloody racehorse.

"Get. Naked." My voice resembled sandpaper on a blackboard and he laughed.

"Not today, sweetheart. If you want me, we'll be taking this slow." If he'd doused me with icy water, it couldn't have been more effective at killing the mood.

"What?" I tugged away, more than a little aware my entire body was rosy with passion.

"I don't do fast and you deserve some slow courting." His eyes may be passion-glazed but they were also firm.

"I… uh…" Well, that left me stuck for words.

"Go back to your room. Dress and we'll find a late lunch. Maybe go for a walk. Hold hands and make out for a while?" He sounded earnest and for the first time, I wanted that. I didn't mistake the fact I was also horny, but that I could probably deal with in the privacy of my room. "Okay. I need to shower first."

I caught up the wrap I'd ditched on his floor, cinched it tight and scooped up my bra. I'd be needing it later, I guessed as I headed for my room. My battery-operated boyfriend was waterproof, and it was about to get a work out, since Charlie wasn't yet ready to go all the way.

CHAPTER 4

I felt like an idiot, waiting for Amanda to emerge from her room. Standing there, as people sauntered by. I know more than one took a look at me and must have been wondering if I was some kind of groupie.

I knew she had them. I'd seen the pics on the internet.

Sighing, I was ready to sit on the floor when her door opened and out stepped Amanda. Her dress red and green was almost Christmas festive. It sat at knee length with a slight flare and the strappy sandals she'd chosen to go with it bared her toes.

"Miss Amanda Symons, will you allow me to escort you?" God, the words nearly stuck in my throat, but she smiled, shy and almost bashful.

"Why, I'd be honoured, kind sir." We stepped down into the lobby and into a raucous mess of gathered media.

"Hey Amanda," one of the photographers called, and I turned, blinked with the flash of the light.

"Who's the stiff?" called another.

My blood started boiling but the hotel security was already there, ushering the media from the door. "Who the fuck let them in?" I roared and the young desk clerk scurried over, her face a picture of remorse.

"I'm soooo sorry. I don't know how they got wind of her being here. We kept everyone's identities quiet. Someone talked, but it wasn't me and I don't think anyone from the hotel. I've already spoken to the manager and he's going to deal with it." The girl implored, as if willing us to understand. It wasn't her fault, I knew that, but right now, our date… Our *first* date was ruined.

I felt the convulsive clutch of her hand on my arm. "It's okay, Charlie. We can go into the dining room. Perhaps they'll arrange a table for us." Her voice soothed the ragged edges of my mind. I felt the shake of her hands and slipped mine over hers.

"No, I shouldn't have lost my temper," I added well aware I may have over reacted. It's just, in my mind this event, special and private, was meant to be just for us. Now some idiot with a telephoto lens and overactive social media account would likely have it on the evening news.

Fuck!

We headed for the dining room and the head waiter was very welcoming, setting us up a quiet corner, complete with large plants so we'd be almost alone. It wasn't what I hoped for and ideas of making out while cuddling her close against the cold weather frittered away like sand on the beach.

I ordered wine and it arrived. Upgraded, the waiter insisted and on the house. The cut glass of bubbles pressed into our hands.

Tiny canapes came out though Amanda looked at them with a sigh. "Wish I could, but dieting's a bitch."

"Sure," I answered and felt like an idiot.

"This isn't the way either of us expected it to go," she started, and I shook my head. "I guess I thought, initially when we were kids, a movie, shared popcorn and you know… As we got older, I thought perhaps dinner, dancing and some light petting." She looked around the room.

I cleared my throat.

"You're uncomfortable with me talking about sex, aren't you, Charlie. Why is that?"

I know my face flamed because the heat scorched my cheeks. "I'm not uncomfortable with it, per se. It's just in public like this doesn't feel very appropriate. It's a private thing."

"I think being so long in the modelling world had made me release inhibitions. I'm sorry I'm making you uncomfortable. What I did find out, when I headed back to the bathroom before, was there is a private viewing platform on the roof. We could head up there."

Her suggestion, privacy and quiet appealed on every level to me. "Do you want to?"

She leaned in and smiled. "I'd do just about anything, including finding myself in your bedroom. Oh, that's right, I already did that." Her teasing tone made me shiver. Anticipation with her was just perfect, I decided, though maybe I wouldn't last too long.

The dining room was long behind us as we started up the steps, four flights of narrow stone. She shivered, with the cold I guessed, and I dragged her close. The door was new and smelled of paint, with an exit light illuminated above it. With a careful push, I opened the door and we arrived at the private lookout.

A long bench sat against the railing to one side and a table and chairs to the other. It was windy, snapping at hour hair and Amanda kept pushing at strands that whipped to and fro. It annoyed her but I find it very human. More like the girl I'd known in the past.

She moved to the edge, her arms resting on the old stonework parapet and gazing into the distance. The sea battered at the rocks and the land. Primal. Untamed.

"Like what you see?" I whisper in her ear, bracketing my body around hers and protecting her from the worst ravages of the wind.

She turns in my arms. "Exceptional," she answers, and we kiss. It's hot and banking the fires proves more than a little difficult.

"Well, what about the view," I sputter willing the ever-present erection to subside to a comfortable level.

She turns back and gazing out there. "It's wonderful. Nothing to tame it. Nothing to still it." While she's talking though, she's grinding her hips against me and I have to close my ease and think cold thoughts of ice-cream, icicles and cold showers. *Nope, not working.*

I'm hard like a spike and fucking needy. *Maybe you are, but you've set the agenda, dimwit. So, suck it up like a man.* I can't help but poke at her with my dick, and she smothers a laugh.

"You'll need to try harder," and she whoops with laughter, "otherwise everyone will think they know what we're up to."

I wish it were that simple. Closing my eyes for a moment, I'm battling for control. I think about Brutus, the wedding cake disaster, Riley and Netta.

Sure, I'd finally controlled myself, I exhale, straighten my shoulders and prepare to utter my pre-rehearsed lines.

"Amanda,"

The beautiful woman before me turns back and stops my words before I can even form them in my mind.

"Later. Whatever you want to say or ask, leave it til later. Let's just be."

I gaze into her eyes. The distance between us not far enough to banish thoughts of sex and forever.

She's not ready. I'm not either, so I keep my counsel, even though it physically pains to do so.

When she drops her head onto my shoulders, for a moment the world feels right. Complete.

The sunlight is fading now, and I clear my throat. "We should find out what time dinner is."

She startles. "Damn. I'm supposed to ring Patrick."

I arch my brow. "Patrick?"

"My agent," she answers, and we retreat. At our doors I stop her. I'm not going to kiss her, here and now. I know she wants it, but I want just a little longer to bask in the privacy of being an unknown couple. It won't last long. Hell, probably everyone already knows, but I can fool myself for maybe another few hours.

"Sit next to me at dinner?"

She nods and we part.

CHAPTER 5

I'm no idiot. I can read a room from a hundred paces. A skill that's assisted me in my modelling career. Tonight, I can see *they all know about us.*

Beforehand, any guy I was seen with, the ones that made a show, the ones who didn't because they knew they were important? It didn't matter. They handled themselves and I left them to do it.

I'm good at putting on a show. Especially the goofy 'I'm just a model, so don't get too excited about anything I say'. With Charlie it's all different.

I sit down beside the magazine's art director, ensuring there's a spot for Charlie. When he wanders in ten minutes later, I can hear the ripple of conversation.

They were seen together entering the lobby.

An affair?

Who is he?

Anger strikes deep. How dare they question him and his value. I want to stand and yell at them all. He's so damned much better than them all.

Charlie won't thank me for that, so I keep my frustration to myself as he settles himself beside me. Under the table, our hands link, for just a moment. Enough to satisfy the urgent need for a physical connection.

He touches my leg with his and I turn, my eyebrows arching.

I read the question in his eyes and answer with a tiny shake of my head. The last time I played footsie with someone I fell off the chair, knocked the table flying and almost caused an international incident.

Been there. Done that. Thank heavens I don't have the prison t-shirt to prove it!

The first course comes out, and I enjoy the soup. It's warm and familiar. It's replaced by a terrine of pheasant, served with seasonal root vegetables in a light sauce. Nice, but I stick to the veggies and try only a little bit of the meat.

Keeping my figure is becoming more and more of a trial these days. Gone are the days when I could eat what I wanted and not have to exercise. Now it's an hour of cardio and crunches and watching what I inhale, let alone consume.

My days of headlining are coming to an end and I need to keep working for at least another year or two. Then I can retire. Open a bookstore if I like... *and I do...* until retirement when I'm ready. I have no interest in handling a herd of young models, like so many of my counterparts do when they retire from modelling. It's not really my game.

The dinner drags on. I turned to the manager and she smiled. "So, I guess you'll be more than happy to model for us again next year. Since you're nearing retirement, you'll be willing to consider a cut in your fees, right?"

Shock coursed through me. *A cut?* Before I could answer, Charlie covered my hand with his. "We'll see. It depends on what we're both doing this time next year."

The woman's eyes grew large. Like, *'holy shit, did you just sorta drop you're an item,'* kind of wonder staring out at me.

"Well," she breathed. "We can always discuss this in the lead up to next year's planning."

By now I'm ready to get out of here and turn back to Charlie. "I don't do dessert. Too many calories."

He blinked and I shot up, then had to admit surprise when he followed me. Dozens of eyes watched as we walked from the dining room, but back in the lobby I turned. "Why did you do that?"

His face tightened. "She wanted to use you. Thought you'd be cheaper next year. They've already approached me about providing the jewellery again... for a fee." He grimaced. "It's not like they're asking for a cut price range. We represent exceptional value. We give them a range to use for competition purposes, we pay to be included. Yes, we gain international coverage, but nothing about this is free for us."

I gulped, understanding what he was saying, but it didn't make it easier to hear.

"All of us are paying huge amounts. Then they want to go all cut price with you? No, Amanda. They want your services and expertise, they should pay well for it."

How could I not appreciate this man? He treated me with respect and I... Oh man, this was huge! I loved him. I loved him for the care he showed me. I loved him because he appreciated me for me!

But saying the words? Well, that was another thing. "I..." the word resembled the croak of an ugly fat frog and he cupped my cheek with his hand.

"Trying to say something?"

I nodded, furious with myself but needing to tell him exactly what was there. "I want...." Clearing my throat, I wondered just how I could push them out.

"Come on." He towed me across the lobby and up to the hallway. Outside our rooms, he stopped, kissed me. Soft. Chaste.

God damn it!

With a hint of laughter in his eyes, he plucked my keys from my hands, inserted it into the lock and shoved me inside. I turned, ready to tug him in but he stepped back. "Sleep well and think of me."

He closed the door and there I was alone. No man ever left me alone like this. What the hell was going on?

The fire inside me urged that I should open the door, pound on his until he let me in then give him a night of unimaginable pleasure.

My brain said, 'whoa girl, slow those horses.' For some reason, my brain won.

The small phone, discarded on the bedside table beeped and I picked it up. Peered at the screen. Media enquiries.

I could answer them. It's what Patrick would want me to do, but this time, I didn't. Instead I turned it off. Tomorrow would be soon enough.

Stalking around the room while my entire body burned with need wasn't the best plan in the world. For some weird reason, I was sure this was the only way forward if I wanted a happy ever after with Amanda.

She was next door.

She wanted me.

If all I wanted was sex, I'd have been through that door faster than a mosquito on uncovered skin.

I wanted more, though. Live the Happy Forever After in all the storybooks.

Sleep was going to be a hell of a long time coming and I turned, inspecting the room for something, anything to do.

I spied the desk, old and heavy dark wooded. The lamp with the bendy metal neck, allowing me to direct where it shone. An idea flashed. Perfect and complete it came. A rose, with a small winking ruby set in the middle.

The trunk sat in the middle of the room. I opened the heavy leather lid and reached inside to retrieve my working mat, pliers and wire of platinum. A small ruby winked by the light perfect for my needs.

How to achieve it? I reached for the soldering iron and medium, as the knowledge poured through me. I allowed myself to be in the moment, consumed by the vision that drove me on, and when I finally sat back, inspected my efforts there lay a tiny yet perfect rose on the mat.

I reached for a box, scooped the tiny item up and slid it inside. It wouldn't be for the magazine. This would be a gift. One of love.

Satisfied with tonight's efforts I stepped away from the table, headed for the bathroom to wash then flopped onto the bed. Closing my eyes, I fell into a deep and dreamless sleep.

The cup of tea in my hands had long since grown cold and I glanced once more in the direction of the doorway.

I'd never known Charlie to pass up breakfast. All his favourites— *cholesterol loaded, yet they smelled so good*—lined up in a stunning array of choices.

I stood and excused myself from the table and was headed for his door when he lumbered down the steps. Rings under his eyes but when he raised his glance to me, I saw a happy smile on his lips.

Would I ever get used to this?

His hand reached for mine and my palm warmed. "Good morning," I said.

"Not bad, though I could think of something that would make it perfect."

The lurch of my heart warned me to be careful, but oh how I wanted to respond with some teasing remark. Maybe along the lines of, "well, if you'd let me in last night, I could have made it happen."

His eyes glinted, his smile became a grin and I realised I'd spoken aloud. "Shit!"

Laughter crinkled the corners of his eyes. "Potty mouthed in the morning, are you?"

I'd always been so good keeping my thoughts to myself. If I hadn't, I never would have made it as far as I had. Trust me, models hear and see things all the time, and it takes a great amount of self-control not to say what came to mind!

At least I hadn't yet told him I thought of him like sex on a stick… A very well packaged one at that!

"Breakfast is almost over."

"Well, we better get in there now, hadn't we?" He took my hand and towed me back into the dining room just as the waiter took my cup of tea.

"Well damn," I uttered, and he questioned my comment with his eyes. "They just took my cup of tea."

"Then we'll get you a new fresh and hot one. See if we can find some of those little biscuit things you usually nibble for breakfast too."

I stared, unaware he knew my morning habits. "Your dad was having trouble before the end tracking them down. He asked me to get a supply in for you."

Tears pricked my eyes as grief washed over me. To the very end, Dad was still trying to look after me.

"Thank you." I touched his arm before turning away. At the server's station I enquired about the breakfast offerings and the server dragged a box out from under the cloth.

"We get them in every year. You models all tend to eat the same things," he laughed.

I settled at an empty table for four, a plate with four tiny squares of dry biscuit and a cup of tea and waited. Charlie joined me, his plate piled high with scrambled eggs, bacon, tomato and tiny sausages.

My stomach grumbled as the scent of it drove me wild.

Once I've stopped modelling, then, stomach, you're going to be re-acquainted with those scrummy flavours!

It must have been loud, because Charlie looked to me. "Want some?"

I waved the offer away, not sure I could push the lie of 'no,' out between stiff lips.

Charlie stared for another couple of moments then shrugged, cut a bite of sausage and popped it in his mouth. I watched him eat, the way his perfect lips surrounded the meat and I have to be honest, I may have sighed a little bit.

His gaze captured mine and the heat of a blush filled me.

He knew. I could tell, the way his lips curved then he winked.

Who knew Charlie could be such a tease?

With the meal finished, we rose and headed to our rooms. I'd clean my skin and scoop up my bag once I'd cleaned my teeth. At the door we parted, and I hurried, blanking out thoughts of him, because if I didn't god knew, I'd need my B.O.B. again... Right now, it had seen two uses in under twenty-four hours and I'd never really been a sexual creature.

The carry on with the Latin guy? Yeah, we'd agreed to behave as we had, and his girlfriend had been one of the directors for the shoot had assisted, taking the photos and 'leaking' them to the media.

It had been mutually beneficial. They'd wanted to smother some of the heat they were getting from his parents, who wanted him to 'experience the world before settling down.' After that, they'd gladly welcomed her because, what parents needed to think their son was some kind of loose gigolo? I'd been the Maid of Honour at the wedding five months ago, his parents had been frigidly stiff, but meh, the party had been phenomenal.

I'd appreciated the opportunity to end it with Marty because I'd known, almost as soon as that ring had slipped onto my finger that I'd made a huge mistake and couldn't think of a nice way to squirm out of it without hurting his feelings.

Without a thought, I left my room and headed for the grand ballroom, where the scene was being set. A room to the side became a dressing room and storage for the dressings to be used for the photos. Racks of gowns, lingerie and so one waited. A team of makeup specialists laid out brushes and pots, while the mirror and lighting shone bright.

A hairdresser, one well versed in her craft took up another corner of the room. I knew this would be the same in several other small rooms on this floor. The other models and the headlining guy would each need their own space.

I settled into the hairdresser's chair and let her work, felt the tug and play of hands, before I was turned, sitting in the foundation garments for the first shoot. Gowns. My least favourite article in these events.

A nail technician buffed and primed my nails as the makeup was applied, then finally it was done.

A cry went up.

I shot from the chair wondering what the hell was happening as the sound of raised voices filled the air. I stopped at the door to see Sergio, my male equivalent stalking down the hall. "No! I will not do that. I quit!" Each of his words rose higher and higher until it became a screech.

Such a drama queen. Hell, queen was it. His boyfriend, Tomas had been getting more and more frustrated as Sergio was photographed with women on his arm and in the magazines. They'd kept it under wraps because who wanted to know that Sergio, one of the sexiest men alive was really gay? It was a well-known fact in the industry and one he used well and to his advantage.

Tomas was lovely if a little needy, and it still astounded me that he'd taken up with the highly strung man. I shrugged then considered. If Sergio had quit who would they get to…

The art director came hurrying into my room, her eyes wheeling with horror. "Sergio's just quit on us and is leaving. We need a male headliner. Who do you know that might be available?"

I ran through the list of men I knew who'd experience but they were either busy or on holidays.

Charlie wandered into the room and it hit me, just like a lump of wood over the back of my head. Charlie. *Sweet, sexy Charlie.* The man with hands of a craftsman and the face of an angel.

"How about Charlie?" The words slipped out and I wasn't in the least bit guilty I'd said his name. Why? Because he was downright gorgeous and would be perfect in the role.

The art director turned as Charlie stared at her. "What?" Horror laced his tone.

The woman walked around him, sizing him up like a hotdog ready for a bun.

"Sergio, our male headliner just quit. We need a male, someone tall, dark and good-looking to step in," the woman said.

I grinned when he looked stunned. "But…"

The woman grabbed him. "How tall are you?"

"Six foot four," he stuttered, and she hurried off.

Charlie stared at me. "What the hell just happened?"

I stepped forward but before I could kiss him, the makeup artist thrust herself between us. "Don't you dare ruin the makeup!"

People rushed in, and Charlie was tugged away from the room, while the art director huddled in the corner, phone to her ear, renegotiating for everything she was worth. Granted, Christina's pretty good at what she does, though has no sense of humour.

I watched, pleased that I wasn't the centre of the drama unfolding.

It felt like an hour, though I knew they'd worked like demons before we both stood in the ballroom again, me in a fluffy poufy gown, a tiara in my hair and Charlie being led in, his face confused while they positioned him.

I couldn't help my grin. "How're you feeling?"

"Afraid," he growled. "They wanted to put padding in my underwear." He sounded aggrieved and I know my brows shot up.

He didn't need any assistance in that area, I already knew, the memory of our bodies nestled together running through my mind.

I had to clear my throat because I was starting to feel that heated passion burning inside me again. Damned inconvenient timing, if you asked me.

The photographer called out, "she's overheating, we need the air-conditioners!"

I wanted to crawl into a hole in the ground, because I wasn't overheating. I was blushing and turned on and the photographer couldn't tell the difference!

Charlie growled deep in his throat every time they repositioned him. "I don't know how you do this day in and day out."

For the first time I considered what he said, the way they touched me like I was a mannequin. Before, it hadn't really occurred to me I didn't like it, but today it felt odd. Strange.

I changed from the poufy confection into a sheath of white silk.

He changed into a dove gray suit and the whole time all I could think was, how he'd helped me out, when the jeweller they'd lined up pulled out in the other shoot. Now he was doing me a favour. A huge one. Was this how it was going to be? One sided with him giving and giving and giving and me just taking?

I didn't like the way my thoughts were headed, so concentrated on my task, ensuring I didn't smile too widely, act like a wooden robot and all the other things I'd learned over the years.

By the time the lunch break was called, I'd used up most of my well of calm and waited as my dress was stripped from me.

Next up was the lingerie shoot. At least it would be a closed room for that. If Charlie wasn't around, I might just be able to regain my equilibrium.

A tray of fruits and salads arrived, water and juice too.

Yep, hiding sounded really good right about now, so I closed the door and settled at the table until it slid open, Charlie striding inside.

"What's up?" His demand took me by surprise.

"What do you mean?" I kept my voice neutral, my eyes wide with faux surprise.

"Don't start that with me," he said and plonked himself onto the chair opposite me. "I've always been able to read you. You're hiding something."

The silence stretched.

He was right, but how could I explain why I was hiding my true emotions. That great big 'L' word reverberated in my brain. The one I was trying to ignore right now, but it hung around like a bad smell, reminding me of my cowardly status.

"I don't know what you mean," I croaked.

He sprang forward and kissed me. All my defences shattered under the onslaught of his mouth on mine. The scent of him in my nostrils and my body reacting as he moved against me.

An involuntary moan filled the air and I recognised the sound as my own.

When he drew away, I was reduced to a mass of quivering nerves and passionate hunger.

"Well," he said. "That's better."

I stared. "Better?" The word sprang from my lips, while my mind struggled to understand what had just happened.

"Yes. The natural you is what I need."

He grinned and I stared because, well, I mean... *What the hell?* "Natural?"

"Yes." The word he repeated hung in the air between us, alongside the 'L' word and the situation we found ourselves in.

I stood, then sat back down. "Who do you think you are?" I tried to summon up a well of anger but it melted pretty damn quick when he stood, tugged me up and into his arms.

"I'm the man you're seriously thinking of starting a relationship with. Remember yesterday, in my room, when you all but stripped me naked?"

How could I? After all, I'd been so hot and out of control I'd had to do something solo to settle myself.

His breath skittered along my nerves, as his lips found the skin of my temple. "I want you."

His hand found mine and he slid it over the erection I could feel through the pants of the grey suit he wore.

Man! He was hard and ready. My nipples pebbled and that bloody hunger coursed through my veins like quicksilver.

A knock at the door sounded and we sprang apart like two horny teenagers on my parents' couch! The art director walked in. "We're going to change the plan. The lingerie shoot will be tomorrow morning. Instead, we're going to do the jewellery shoot this afternoon. You're going to need to wear the casual choices first, while we focus on the engagement rings."

I gulped. I'd seen the plan for the engagement shoot. The plan was Sergio sliding the ring onto my finger. There was far too much involved now for me to see it as anything other than just another shoot. After all, this would be Charlie and I.

I nodded, unable to form the words that might herald the fact that I was uncomfortable.

Charlie watched my face as the director left the room. "What was that all about?"

"Ahhh... The shoot is going to need you sliding rings onto my hands. I think there's about seven, right?"

For a moment his face took on that blank unfocussed look then he smiled. "Sure, why not?"

He left the room and I stared after his retreating back wondering what the hell was going on now. After all, here I was dealing with the emotional strain of him sliding a ring on my finger, when in actual fact it's what I craved in real life.

CHAPTER 6

Sliding a ring on her finger. I hurried back to the room, wondering about the sanity of what I was considering. Sliding open the bedside drawer, my eyes settled on the small leather case.

Excitement warred with terror. Was it too much too soon? We'd known each other for a lifetime, yet we'd not been intimate. I knew how I felt, but she hadn't said the words to me, nor had I said them to her.

Like the ring, the case had been carefully crafted. The soft calfskin leather, and silk lining cradled the token of my love. I opened the lid and looked at the creation inside, checking the sparkle and shine, then shut the box. Without allowing myself time to even think, I slipped the package into my pants pocket and returned to the ballroom.

"Good. Now come this way," I was urged and followed the directions of the photographer.

Amanda was waiting there, her face pale and wrapped in a wine-red evening gown. We were led to a table, set for a meal complete with candlelight.

They shoved a ring into my hands, and I took my time. Giving it a last rub to shine it up.

I didn't look at Amanda's face, just concentrated on the task.

Music piped, something quiet and classical, the air cooler than previously even with the artificial lighting.

The photographer and his assistant staged both of us, the ring. The way it slid onto her finger amid the continuous clicks of the camera.

We changed to a second ring, larger and the wrong style for Amanda. This time I looked up, saw the stunned look on her face and hated the setting right now.

The crew stopped and huddled together. "I'm sorry about this," I murmured, well aware of the agitation that coiled her tight. Saw the brackets at her mouth from strain.

"It's okay," she answered but the tone was stretched as if she didn't want to be here. Nerves quivered and jumped inside me as the weight in my pocket mocked me.

The session resumed, more ideas and suggestions, further poses. We came to the final ring and I halted them all, wishing them to perdition and me as well. They might have been my designs, but they weren't anything I'd choose for this woman. They didn't come close to capturing her essence.

I was called over and handed yet another ring. The photographer gave me a funny look and I bent over her hand. "Hmm, let me give that a shine."

I reached into my pocket, the case rubbing against my fingers. Did I dare? On a split-second decision, I slipped my fingers past it and pulled out a cloth. "It's got a fingerprint," I added.

She nodded, and sighed. I gave it a shine then we parted, ready to start the next part of the charade. Amanda came out moments later, dressed in one of the gowns. The lacey confection close to the one she'd worn for the recent and somewhat disastrous shoot. My lips curved into a smile at the memory of what had occurred. Funny how time dulled the sharp edges, I mused.

This time when Amanda gazed at me, I could see the return of the mirth, as we both recalled her in that silly dress. Memories of her keeping the pouf down out of her face, driving her car rolled around in my mind and I laughed, then was shushed by one of the assistants.

"Are they always this tough?" I questioned.

"Sometimes it's worse. Gerald and Suzi are cross because Sergio walked out and they'd spent hours going over the set ups with both of us, so we knew the shots they needed. Having to bring in someone cold, and without the experience is making it take a whole heap longer."

I considered this. There was clearly an art to modelling. It was one I hadn't mastered and doubted I'd like to.

"Meet me afterwards, in one of those sexy lingerie get up's," I whispered and watched as her eyes widened.

Then the photographer bellowed, "light check," and I set my mind to the shoot once more.

The photoshoot was beyond painful! I mean, the whole time I was supposed to be thinking about the angles and positions, the lights and how to convey the emotion of joy was overridden by my confusion at Charlie's last words. *'Meet me afterwards, in one of those sexy lingerie get up's.'* What did he expect me to do with that?

Gerald and Suzi rode my ass like a donkey on the Grand Canyon, because my head certainly wasn't in the game. In the end, the session took twice as long as planned, I felt like a whipped cream dessert and meanwhile, Mr 'sexy lingerie' Charlie watched me like I was a candy on a stick.

I was out of sorts, frustrated—and yes, both mentally and sexually —by the time they released me from the afternoon's torture, and I may have stalked to my room in a foul mood. Meanwhile, Charlie being the afternoon's teacher's pet was released much earlier. He'd left and I had no idea where he'd gone. "So much for the sexy lingerie idea," I muttered as I let myself into my room, then stopped.

Shock skittered through my system as I stared, the door banging closed behind me. I barely noticed it, because there was Charlie, reclining on my bed. Flowers littered surfaces I hadn't expected and a meal waiting on a candlelit table.

Soft music crooned and my breath caught. Two champagne flutes waited, bubbles of effervescence rising to the surface.

Scent. Sound. Sight.

"Charlie?" It was all I could manage as I stood there.

He rose and advanced. "I wanted to give you something no one else had."

I gaped, probably looking like a fish out of water. "I..."

Charlie drew me into his arms, his lips finding mine in a tender kiss. One that drugged and promised things I didn't really expect would ever be mine.

When he moved away, my body mourned the loss of his heat.

An impudent smile crept over his face, and it captured me and my attention.

"I thought an intimate dinner for two, wearing something special." His fingers moved to the buttons of his shirt and with the sound of each popping free from the holes the heat that constantly licked at my insides grew, smothering any kind of thought.

His shirt swung open and I noted the sculpted chest and abdomen I'd only glimpsed irregularly.

"Join me, Amanda." The throaty invitation set those fires licking at the most secret recesses of my body.

"I..." The croaking of my voice was hardly romantic, yet his grin grew larger.

When his hands reached for his belt a lump lodged itself in my throat. "What...?"

"Lingerie," he whispered and when his pants hit the floor my eyes were drawn to his groin.

The bulge I'd felt appeared bigger than ever before and, Lord, the urgency to shove him back to the bed and ride him like a pogo stick almost shattered me.

"Amanda?" He reached out with both hands, pulled me close against his now almost nude body. Only his dick and balls covered with black silk and my fingers itched to strip that silly bit of material off him.

I felt him reach, heard the sound of the zip on my dress sliding down and the sudden gape of my dress left me in no doubt what he was doing. When he slid the shoulders of the gown over my arms, I let him.

Cool air blew over exposed skin, because all I wore was a tiny demi bra and G-string.

I heard his breath, drawing in.

"You said…" I cleared my throat, well aware my body betrayed my sudden arousal, "You said to wear lingerie. So, I did."

I glanced at his face and the smile of masculine satisfaction was like adding coal to a furnace… as in the one chugging out heat in my gut! I cleared my throat again. "I see you organised dinner."

Taking my hand, he pulled me to the table, and I wondered what on earth he planned now. I heard his hiss, and smiled at him, aware that the sight of my bare backside left him more than a little interested, if the swelling of that bulge in his underwear was correct. My fingers curled inwards as I fought the instinctive desire to caress the contents of that black silk.

"Not now," he whispered and the whisper of his breath over my shoulder and throat stole my senses.

Charlie pushed me down onto the one of the velvet covered chairs and I groaned as the material caressed my overly sensitive skin.

He lifted the large metal dome from the plate, and I saw the food he'd arranged for our dinner and laughed. "Fish and chips?"

Charlie sighed. "I was too late to order a three-course meal. It was all they could do on short notice."

The food could have been saw-dust as we ate in silence. The flicker of the candles, the tart bite of the champagne and the sweet taste of the fish lulling me.

I smiled at him. He grinned at me. "Wow, it's been such a long time since I ate a meal like that."

"I guessed," and he softened the words with a gentle slide of his finger over the back of my hands.

In that moment, there was no question in my mind. If he asked me, should that ever occur I'd say yes. I stretched out my hand. "We used to eat this with your parents on the beach."

He nodded. "We did. That's when I first knew."

I blinked. "What?"

"That I wanted to marry you."

That punch of awareness nearly knocked me flat. "What?"

He stood up, the chair grinding across the floor as he moved to his pants, hunted through the pockets then grunted.

The silence drew out has he stepped up to my seat, the black silk of his silly underwear deflated as he stumbled to one knee.

My hand fluttered over my chest and the incongruity of the situation, the way we were dressed pounded at my brain.

"Amanda, I've loved you for years. Watched you grow and become who you are and appreciated the woman you hid from everyone else. Marry me and save my sanity and heart, because without out that, I'm only going through the motions of life."

I stared. Yup. The sexiest, most heartfelt and downright stupidly romantic proposal and I was tongue-tied.

His gaze was earnest but much as I wanted to answer, that damned lump in my throat defeated me. Instead I nodded like a loon, while he knelt on the floor in sexy black underwear!

"The words would be great," he gritted out.

A laugh of embarrassment shoved itself past the blockage. "I guess I should say yes then."

"Only if you want to," Charlie told me, and when I gazed into his eyes, there was fear there.

I reached out, touched his cheek. "Yes, Charlie. I will marry you." Just as I started up out of my seat to slide into his arms, he stilled me. "What?"

"I have something for you," and opened a box, to display the most beautiful ring I'd ever seen. The white metal gleamed in the light and the diamond winked this way and that.

"It's gorgeous."

He slid it onto my finger, and I marvelled at the fit. "I borrowed one of your rings. Your Dad saw it before he died and gave me his permission."

Tears burned the inside of my lids. "My Dad knew?"

Charlie nodded. "Yeah, I spoke to him a year or two ago. He gave his permission and said he hoped one day you'd realise a good man waited for you."

I launched into Charlie's arms then, my lips squeezed against his.

He stumbled and I fell over him. A limpet hanging onto life because the ground felt like it shifted beneath me, metaphorically speaking, of course.

When Charlie rolled, I let him. He leaned over me and his gaze darkened with raw sensuality. "Well now, that little thing isn't doing its job, now is it?"

Sometime during the jump and roll, my bra had shifted, and I'd been, let's just say, uncovered.

I tittered. Yup, that funny little laugh escaped until his hand found my breast and touched it gently. His hands weren't smooth and perfect like those of my other lovers. They were scarred and ridged from burns and metal cuts but they touched me with exquisite gentleness.

I gasped then and his hands slid away, pushing beneath me and wrestling with the clip of my bra. I felt it give and let him slide it from my body, releasing my breasts to his wondering gaze.

"So damned beautiful," then he kissed me, and my body felt the slide of nipples against bare naked torso. My body demanded more, and I reached up, found the stupid silk that covered him and slid my fingers below.

"Wait," Charlie groaned. "Give a guy a minute."

A minute might be more than I could manage, as I wheezed and puffed oxygen into my lungs. "I need you," I sighed, and his eyes squeezed shut.

"I want to make this last," he groaned, and I giggled hearing the aggrieved tone in his voice.

"Next time," I promised and slipped the silk down over his backside, the tips of my fingers grazing his flesh.

He grunts and rolls me again so I'm on top. I like this position, because now I can feel every glorious inch of him. Squirming ratchets the fire that's scorching deep inside me and I slide. Charlie gasps and I feel the urgent jerk of his erection.

Our lips meet again, as his fingers dig into my scalp holding me close. The fierce mating of our lips little more than a shadow of the need I feel for him.

I pull away, my head thrust back, and his lips fasten against one very hard nipple. "oooohhhh..."

"I want you," he growls against my flesh and I nod, unable to speak because right now he's tearing my panties away, the sound of material rending filling the air then his dick is hot and nudging at me.

I adjust so he can thrust inside me and we're complete.

One.

Full.

So damned full and I'm moving, riding. Undulating over him. Urging him on while I grip him hard, my legs like vices at his hips.

The orgasm screams to life, and I'm gone. Lost in a whirl of lights and sensations, eyes closed tight while I feel him filling me up, ejaculating.

My heart's racing, my chest bellows then calms slowly, and I slump down.

"Wow," he gathers me close and I close my eyes, still aware we didn't even make it to the bed.

"So, I guess now we're official," I offer, the words slurring with the sudden onset of exhaustion.

"I guess we are," he says and rolls enough so he can lift me in his arms and carry me to the bed.

"What happened to take is slow?" I murmur.

He grunts. "That would be silly, wouldn't it?" He tugs me close.

"You've got energy?" I whisper and he kisses my brow as he pulls the sheet over our naked bodies.

"I think that's me done too," he answers.

I'm almost asleep when I hear him whisper against my temple. "Thanks Gus. Once more you were right."

EPILOGUE

The gown is a mermaid style, fitted around my breasts and hips then flaring at the thighs. My makeup flawless and the ring on my finger heavy and sparkling in the light. A tiny rose necklace with a ruby inlaid is my only adornment.

Brutus is on the ground, scratching up a circus of fleas while I'm waiting for the car to arrive.

I refused a veil. I want to see Charlie as I march down the aisle towards him. He's the only man I ever got this far with. I'd made promises to others, but they'd been weak and hadn't stood up to careful inspection, while Charlie... He'd known all my foibles and loved them anyway. It's why I had never married anyone else. "I guess I knew all along," I muttered.

Today we'd marry then I'd give him the envelope that burned in my tiny bridal bag.

Selina crowded close. "How are you feeling? Belly still a bundle of nerves?" She'd sent her twins on with her husband while Mrs Campbell—Miri, as I'd now been instructed to call her — bustled around filling the spot my unlamented and missing mother would never fill.

"Great," I answered but it wasn't exactly the full truth. Nerves knotted me up and I just wanted that car here, right now, so I could walk up to Charlie and marry him. The urgency to say yes growing bigger every moment.

The floral spray of carnation and lily were pressed into my hands and I clutched them, stepping out the doors and into the bright sunshine. Crowds gathered along with craning paparazzi who screamed my name. I ignored them, because today wasn't about them.

The trip passed in a dizzy flash and we were there, at the church. Security was tight…

Everyone except myself and my group had to show id, leave their phones at the door and agree to a non-disclosure agreement. That was the idea of the wedding planner but I'd welcomed it.

Inside the chapel the air was cool, and it washed over my skin as I waited for the music to announce my arrival. It swelled, and everyone stood as I moved forward, my heart keeping time with the music while I drew closer to Charlie waiting at the altar. He looks so handsome in his suit.

His face betrays his amazement as I came into view and it tells me I'd surprised him as Brutus led the way.

I'd insisted he should act as the Dog of the Bride, given my father had passed. The tiny note my father, Gus had penned, the one the solicitor had handed me just three days ago, filled me with love for the memory of the man who'd believed in me, stood by me and approved of this match.

At the altar, when the priest asks "Who gives this woman?" both Charlie and I giggled as I slid the tiny holder from Brutus' collar. "My father via Brutus," I answered.

The crowd roars with laughter as I handed it to the priest. Many of those present know our shared history and they get the depth of emotion in my answer.

He read it and laughed. "She's right," he announces and waves the letter around, then the ceremony moves forward at pace.

Once the vows are exchanged, we repaired to the vestry to sign the book and there, I open my bag and hand Charlie the envelope.

"What's this?" He asks and I took a deep breath.

"Open it," I urge.

He did, drawing out two small images.

"What?"

"Remember the castle? The black silk pants and G-string," I whispered.

His grin grew wide. "Well now."

He captured me close and kissed me. Hard.

"Save that for later," Selina pointed out.

"It's a bit late for that," crowed Charlie and passes her the contents of the envelope.

***

I watched my bride as she took her spot on the floor, Brutus beside her, recreating the scene of the photoshoot that would forever seal the deal for me.

No cake this time would come to an unhappy ending as we'd agreed to choose something fun. Balloons filled a large bathtub instead and she winked at me.

I'd thought nothing could surpass the joy of seeing my ring on her finger. I'd been wrong.

The love I'd felt for her, for so long had started out as mooning over the prettiest girl in the neighbourhood, grown into something deeper than friendship and over time had been infused with a fair dose of lust. But the love had weathered everything from other people, engagements and distance. It brought us full circle, he thought.

Lost in my reverie, I didn't notice the bride grabbing something wet and spongy and throwing it at me.

"What?"

"Concentrate," she laughed, and I did, aware she'd released Brutus who'd started nosing around among the balloons. The popping sound and echoes of laughter behind us reminding me now wasn't the time to ravish my bride.

Cameras clicked, capturing the moment then she rose and walked into my arms.

"I have everything I could ever dream of," I whispered to her.

She laughed. "A Brutus, a bride and a bundle of fun coming soon."

I kissed her and held on tight. Because anything worth keeping is worth holding close.

Did you enjoy Imogene's book? Why not check out some more of her titles, by turning the page!

INHERITANCE OF THE BLOOD BY IMOGENE NIX

In the darkness evil waits...

As a young bride Kira was whisked away from everything and everyone she knew, including her new husband and became Christina, an operative of the Displaced Persons Unit.

As the danger grows she sees an opportunity to save her husband Vasya and sister Serina. But nothing is the same. Serina is grown up—married and pregnant.

Vasya too is older and darkly forbidding. Trusting Christina doesn't come easily until a catastrophic event takes place. Now, knowing the truth everything he thought he knew is changed. But at a very high cost.

The four must work together to defeat the Demon, Zuor and the stakes are higher than they imagined and all could be lost.

The burning at the back of her neck warned she was being watched. A quick glance didn't clarify it. Instead, she turned around in time to see her mother's face, pale. "Mama?"

She took a step forward, but her grandfather snatched her wrist.

The grip was painful, and Kira stilled. "Let your parents talk."

She didn't know what the topic of conversation was, but it couldn't be good.

The dappled sunlight seemed cooler than before.

Her father crooked his forefinger at her grandfather while they stood there. For a moment she wished Vasya had come with them, but he had to work. Just the thought of her new husband warmed Kira.

She only had a few minutes to contemplate her newly defined status as a married woman, when her grandfather pulled at her hand. "Come with me." He tugged and, confused, Kira allowed herself to be towed away.

A glance at her parents' faces stole any feeling of well-being.

"Grandfather?"

"Shh, my love. You must go." His grip was implacable and his face stern, but he shivered.

"What are you doing? Where are you taking me, Grandfather?"

They moved rapidly through the village they'd visited to sell their wares just that morning, and for the first time since they'd arrived in the market place she felt fear. What was wrong? Was it something to do with Vasya?

"You are in danger. We must send you away." The words confused her further. Send her away? Danger?

"Where is Vasya?" She stumbled over a stone, but he kept tugging her onwards.

With a quick glance around, he hauled her into a dirty laneway between the buildings. Kira gasped, trying to drag air into her starving lungs. "There's no time. We must get you away."

A nondescript shopfront lay ahead, and he pushed on the door. It rattled and opened with a loud groan. "Andre? Andre, are you here?"

An older man shuffled into the room, bent nearly double from the weight of the load on his back. "Marat? What do you want?"

"My granddaughter. They are coming for her and us. Get her away. Take her now, while you can."

The man's face clouded over. "Are you sure?"

"Grandfather, where is Vasya?" Fright had the blood in her veins pounding.

"Hush, my precious. Andre will see you well." He turned. "Whatever it takes, Andre. Take her now." With surprising speed, her grandfather whirled and was gone.

The man, Andre, eyed her. "Come this way, child. There is no time to be lost."

Eleven years later

The tattoo of her heart and cry of terror woke her, as they usually did. Once again, as she had since that rapid flight from those who sought her, she found herself in a lonely bed. Hundreds of miles away from everything she'd dreamed of, in a house she'd built for them to share. As always, it left her wishing that Vasya had fled with her.

Instead, here she was, exiled without her husband. With a sob, she rolled over and let the tears fall.

Available from Beachwalk Press
books2read.com/IOTB

Direct Autographed Copy
http://bit.ly/2w6g4K6

THE CELTIC CUPID TRILOGY

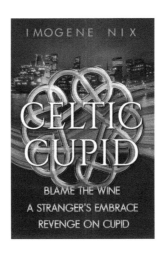

When Cupid—otherwise known as Diocail— is banished from his home on a remote Scottish Island, he's set a series of tasks by the great god Lugh, who also happens to be his father.

In *Blame The Wine*, he must bring two lovers together... BBW Cara and James, the man she's lusted over from afar who happens to be a super geek and head Veha Industries.

In *A Stranger's Embrace*, Diocail is driven to help an emotionally fragile Jane and Davis, a famous author. The task is more complicated, with the existence of Carstairs her could-be ex-husband and teenage daughter, Frannie.

In **Revenge on Cupid**, Diocail must take the ultimate chance and find his own happily ever after with Simone. Sometimes the past gets in the way and HEA's don't come cheap though.

The dusty, dingy little diner was full, even with its current state of cleanliness—or lack thereof. People from the surrounding offices didn't care about anything except the incredible, well-prepared food at a reasonable cost. They flooded in, like waves to the shore. As one tide left, another swept in.

"Honestly, Simone. I'm going to try getting his attention one more time. If that doesn't work, I'm out of there. I mean, how long can I keep trying?" Cara picked at the caramel tart she hadn't been able to resist with the cheap metal fork and flicked the blob of fresh cream that sat on top to the side of the plate.

"You've said that tons of times before. Besides, what are you going to do to get his attention? Hmm? Walk naked through the typing pool?" Simone bobbed the straw in her smoothie as she eyed her friend with a frown. "It's been what? Eighteen months since you saw him, and you've mooned over him from a distance ever since you met him. You need to move on, Cara. That is, unless there's something you haven't shared?"

The query was arch. Cara shivered even as she shook her head. "No."

Simone quirked an eyebrow, obviously unconvinced with the answer. Cara let out a deep sigh of frustration. "There's a position...it's only temporary, for a PA reporting directly to him." She speared a forkful of tart, chewed quickly and swallowed, before continuing. "In his office, full-time for the period of the engagement. I saw the memo yesterday. I mean, I have the skills, right? I can type, answer phones, make coffee, file, greet people. What's more, I can probably do it better than all those size eights in the typing pool that Ms. Jackman seems to prefer." She nodded thoughtfully. "All I have to do is get past the ogre in Human Resources."

Simone stared at her, disbelief clear on her face. "Girl, I so remember that woman. If you think you can get past her, you're doing better than I ever did. That's why I left Veha Industries, remember? Maybe it's time to haul out your resumé and consider some other options. Look for something better." Simone shook her head and billows of her crimson hair swirled through the still air.

Cara understood Simone only had her best interests at heart. But this time she knew the outcome would be different. Hell, she could feel it in the air. The tingle of expectation.

"Cara, the HR ogre will hang you out for breakfast before she offers you anything like a position in that office. Remember her mantra? Good looks and good work make for a positive workplace!"

Simone didn't sugar-coat anything. It was another great reason for their long- term friendship. Honesty. But Cara didn't want to hear the truth in the statement. Even if it was exactly as her friend said.

Cara nodded quickly. "Yeah, I know, but if I don't try, then I won't know how close I can get to him, right? And the only way to catch his attention is to get past *her* and see him in person." Cara quaked a little at the information she needed to share. The favor she needed to ask. "Anyway, I tidied up my resumé and dropped the application into a memo envelope yesterday, so it's too late to back out now. I mean, fortune favors the brave. Doesn't it? If I don't snag an interview, I'm going to visit the career advisor across the street and register with them." She shrugged. "I'll look for temp work until something more long-term shows up. I can see what they have on offer and well...who knows? Maybe a job with the right boss is just waiting for me. But I'd rather this worked out, to be honest." Her voice trailed off into a whisper. "I really wish he would notice me."

Simone took a long slurp of her banana drink, and Cara noticed her questioning gaze even as she squirmed. Finally, Simone nodded. "It's your funeral. So anyway, you'd better show me this memo if you want me to be a referee for you. I'm guessing that's what you need, right? I'll have to know what I'm supposed to say about you before they ring."

Cara smiled. "Thanks, Simone. I knew I could count on you." She slipped a piece of paper out of her handbag and handed it over. "Sorry it's a bit creased. It was in the bottom of my bag, I stashed it so none of the others from the pool would see. You know how it is."

Available from Love Books Publishing
books2read.com/CelticCupid

Direct Autographed Copy
http://bit.ly/2vs7wtS

BIOCYBE BY IMOGENE NIX

Can a cyber-enhanced warrior and a ship's captain find love together?

Levia Endrado never wanted to be a warrior, but at seventeen she was deemed suitable for battle. After intense training and multiple enhancements, which gave her superior strength and healing ability, she was sent off to defeat the enemy—a killing machine with a mission.

When the war was over, she had to find a new life. At twenty-seven she's a washed-up veteran without a future. Or she was, until she met Sandon Daria.

Serving as a pilot aboard Sandon's spaceship the *Golden Echo* makes Levia long for a different and gentler life. But old hurts and even older enemies aren't so easily forgotten. Particularly when they come back for her.

Sandon is determined to show Levia that she's more than just a BioCybe...she's the woman who completes him. Getting close is just the first step, keeping her alive is an even bigger challenge, but one he's willing to take because the prize is their combined future.

Levia scanned the long line of other hopefuls entering the chamber. The large building in the center of town was cold, and she dragged her wrap around her body, even as she craned her head, looking to the high ceiling. She'd never before had an occasion to enter the testing complex, yet she'd seen the lines of teenagers every time they passed the building.

Once she'd asked her parents why the teens were lined up and her mother's face had shuttered. Her stepfather had just shaken his head and growled. They'd stopped her questions with a carefully uttered, "You'll know soon enough, Levia." The pain in her mother's eyes had been enough to shush her questions. For endless months afterward, her parents had traveled different routes to the educational facility she attended and Levia lost interest in the puzzle of that building.

Now, as she looked around, remembering that long ago spring day, it was her opportunity to find out. But she felt a surge of concern at what lay ahead. She likely wasn't the only one, given that there were probably two to three hundred seventeen-year-olds gathered in the one place. Ahead of her, she caught sight of a couple of girls, their arms linked together and wide smiles on their faces. Scanning the crowd, she became aware that, by far, a majority of those gathered displayed both fear and trepidation.

"All female subjects will enter through doors three, six, and seven. All male subjects will enter through gates four, eight, and ten." The speaker above her was loud, and she jumped before checking the numbers etched on the black metal sign over her head.

The massive doors beside her swung open, and now an uncertain silence reigned. Many of the youngsters hung back, clearly discomforted by whatever testing regime lay ahead. This was where they'd been told their futures would be determined.

"Oh gosh, I hope they only have an aptitude and psych eval. I don't think..." Levia turned to see the white face of the girl behind her. The girl had uttered what many must silently be thinking.

Levia dragged an unsteady breath in, her hand resting flat against the plane of her belly as she looked around. No one had entered yet. It was clear many were on the verge of taking the step, but still they hung back.

She straightened her shoulders. "I'm not afraid." It was always wiser to approach things head-on, she believed. When her biological father had died, she'd been one of the few to view his capsule before it was sent into the massive gray structure built to accommodate those who'd moved onto the next life realm.

Her legs shook as she wobbled toward the entrance. Beyond the doorway, she spied sealed cubicles and her heart stuttered. Why cubicles? Usually testing—med and psych—were in eval-units, hidden only by billowing white curtains. She glanced back, noting that others had taken the first step.

"Move along, subjects." Once again, the androgynous voice of the address system blared.

Of course, given it was her seventeenth anniversary of birth, she was technically considered an adult now.

She thought longingly of baby Rald and her half-sister, Elda, waiting at home for her to return, and the celebrations to be held that night. That made her smile. She would need to make them proud of her.

She entered a row and the tall Educational Specialist, the edu-specs as her peers laughingly called them, stopped her. "Present your credentials to the scanner."

She'd done this many times since the tiny implant had been slipped below the dermal layer of her skin at birth. The small unit in her wrist heated as her details were checked.

"Enter the first cubicle, Levia Endrado, and follow the instructions to complete your assessment."

Thus dismissed, Levia moved to the first unit, laid her palm against the scanner, and the door slid open soundlessly.

"Welcome, Levia Endrado. Take your place in the eval-unit." The soft contralto of the voice echoed after the door closed silently behind her.

"What are you evaluating?" Her voice was breathy, and she peered around.

"Your skills—physical and psychological. Your emotional and medical status. Your educational attainment levels."

It was an answer that shed little insight into the many things she was hungry to know. "Why do all seventeen year olds—"

"Take a seat, Levia. Then we may begin your testing."

If she'd expected an answer, she was sadly mistaken, she considered sourly. She dropped into the seat, the soft leather-like surface molding to her body.

"Levia Endrado, you are required to remove all non-specified apparel."

She jolted in the chair. "It's cold."

"The temperature will be amended. Remove the non-specified apparel."

Her misgivings grew as she dragged off the light wrap she'd brought with her, and then threw it to the floor at the side of the unit.

"We will begin, Levia Endrado. At any time, should you experience any malfunctions of the unit, simply depress the red button." It glowed and she grimaced.

Levia reclined against the chair and waited for the testing to begin.

The first examination was based on her understanding of the

political system, where she saw herself, and her knowledge of the rights and responsibilities accorded through citizenship of both her planet and the commonwealth.

The second test was mathematical and scientific proficiency. It felt like hours had passed by the time she'd finished, and she lay limp on the seat, exhausted.

"Levia Endrado, you may rise. The sanitary unit will emerge once you trigger the yellow button at the door. Should you require refreshment, press the blue button and a restorative will be made available."

"Can I leave?"

"Negative, Levia Endrado. Your needs will be catered for in this capsule."

"Why?" Her voice hitched and true fear rose for the first time. Why did they keep her in the alcove?

"All will be revealed at the end of the testing cycle."

Levia looked at the now empty screen before hurling a curse word. It was met with silence.

The urgent throb of her bladder reminded her that she needed to use the facilities, so, with

a sigh, she rose and clambered from the seat. After attending to the needs of her body, she walked around the unit, peering at the door, but it was obviously programmed remotely. She poked and prodded, but it made no difference. With a huff, she headed back to the chair.

The moment she'd settled in, the viewing screen shone bright. "Welcome back, Levia. The next sequence will evaluate your psychological reflexes, then that will be followed up with the general knowledge portion of the evaluation."

"When can I leave?" It seemed better to ask bluntly, she told herself.

"Once the examination is completed. After the next set of evaluations, you will be subjected to the physical aspect."

"Then I can go home?"

"Levia Endrado, you will now complete the psychological test. This will be undertaken by one of the center's personal evaluators."

She frowned. Personal evaluators? She bit her lip, and the sting reminded her that this wasn't something to joke about. In her seventeen years, she'd only heard of personal evaluators being brought in once before, and that was when one of the girls at her academy had been in a serious accident. Both legs were amputated and her body's ability to keep her alive had been gravely compromised. Her peers had been informed that the girl had requested the assessment before she could request her support systems be disconnected.

"Levia Endrado, are you ready to recommence processing?" The emotionless voice echoed once more and she gulped.

"Yes."

Available from Beachwalk Press
http://www.beachwalkpress.com

Direct Autographed Books
http://bit.ly/BioCybe

ALSO BY IMOGENE NIX

Warriors of the Elector

- Star of Ishtar
- Starline
- Starfire
- Star of the Fleet
- Starburst
- The Star of Eternity

The Star of Ishtar & Starline - Print

Starfire & Star of the Fleet - Print

Starburst & The Star of Eternity - Print

Blood Secrets

- The Blood Bride
- The Illuminated Witch
- The Sorcerer's Touch

The Secrets World:

Blood Secrets

- The Blood Bride
- The Illuminated Witch
- The Sorcerer's Touch

House Secrets

- As Dawn Breaks
- Immortal Consequences
- Edge of Night

All That Glitters - a House Secrets Novella

Danu's Secrets

- The Downfall of Padraic O'Shaunessy
- Unnamed Secrets Book II

The Automaton Series

- Haven House
- Nobel Crest
- Casa Bonita (Coming in 2024)

The Search Duology

- Miss Elspeth's Desire
- Miss Isabelle's Craving

Duology World Novels

- A Very Merry Widow

Reunion Trilogy

- War's End
- The Assassin
- Executing Justice

The Reunion Trilogy in Paperback

Sex Love & Aliens

- Tangled Webs
- False Webs
- Covert Webs

21st Testing Protocol

- Cyborg: Redux
- Children Of A Greater Evil
- When Evil Came To Stay
- Finis: The War To End All Wars

Celtic Cupid Trilogy

- Blame The Wine
- A Stranger's Embrace
- Revenge On Cupid

The Celtic Cupid Trilogy in Paperback

Zombieology

- The Reset
- I Dream of Zombies
- The Six Million Dollar Zombie
- Make Room For Zombies
- Days of Our Zombies
- Unnamed Zobiology title (coming soon)

Knights of Pleasure

- Silken Knights

Single Titles

The Chocolate Affair (also in Print)

Falling In Love Again (Previously A Sapphire For Karina)

BioCybe (also in Print)

Hesparia's Tears (also in Print)

Tomorrow's Promise

A Bar In Paris (also in Print)

Inheritance Of The Blood (also in Print)

The Plan

Loving Memories (also in Print)

Hero of Heartbreak Hill (also in Print)

My One & Only

Curse Bound

Non Fiction

Self Publishing: Absolute Beginners Guide (With Suzi Love)

Written as Ciara Cave

25 Curated Ways To Get Rid Of Telemarketers

Book Signings for Absolute Beginners

ABOUT THE AUTHOR

 Imogene is published in a range of romance genres including Paranormal, Science Fiction and Contemporary. She is mainly published in the UK and USA.

In 2010, Imogene Nix (the pen name not Imogene herself) was born. Imogene sat down and worked tirelessly for 3 months culminating in the book Starline, which became the first in a trilogy titled, "Warriors of the Elector." Since then she's had over 30 titles published and is now focusing on hybridising herself - with a mixture of traditionally published and self-published works.

In fact, she's taking control of many of her back catalogue books, which are slowly re-releasing as self-published titles.

Imogene is a member of a range of professional organisations world wide, and believes in the mantra of mentoring and paying it forward and is actively involved in mentorship (through NaNoWrimo and her vlog: In The Chair With Imogene Nix) and tutoring of new and upcoming authors.

In her spare time she loves to drink coffee, wine & eat chocolate and is parenting her spoiled dog and a ferocious cat along with her family and looks forward to weekends away with her husband in their caravan "The Seven Year Hitch!" Do look forward to her caravan romance at some point!

To Contact Imogene
www.imogenenix.net
imogene@imogenenix.net

facebook.com/ImogeneNix
x.com/ImogeneNix
instagram.com/ImogeneNix
bookbub.com/authors/imogenenix

9 781922 369710